short shorts on family and other issues

by philippa c. jabouin

Copyright © 2022 philippa c. jabouin

All rights reserved. This book may not be reproduced in whole or in part, in any form, or by any means, electronic or mechanical, including photocopying, recording, or by any information storage and retrieval system now known or hereafter invented without permission in writing from the author.

short shorts on family and other issues

ISBN 978-1-7779728-0-6 (Hardcover)

Editors: Christine Bode, Deanna Brannon, and Les éditions subversives

Book production by Dawn James, Publish and Promote

Layout, and interior design by Publish and Promote

Cover artwork by Caroline Lavoie-Gauthier, artiste plasticienne et mosaïste entitled "Sulphurous Exchange"

Printed and bound in Canada

Note to the reader: This is a work of fiction. Unless otherwise indicated, all the names, characters, businesses, places, events and incidents in this book are either the product of the author's imagination or used in a fictitious manner. Any resemblance to actual persons, living or dead, or actual events is purely coincidental. The information is provided for educational purposes only.

For Leïla

TABLE OF CONTENTS

family

Story #1	9
Story #2	11
Story #3	13
Story #4	15
Story #5	17
Story #6	19
Story #7	21
Story #8	23
Story #9	25
Story #10	27
Story #11	29
Story #12	31
Story #13	33

work

Story #14	37
Story #15	39
Story #16	41

Story #17	43
Story #18	45
Story #19	47
Story #20	49

life

Story #21	53
Story #22	55
Story #23	57
Story #24	59
Story #25	61
Story #26	63
Story #27	65
Story #28	67
Story #29	69
Story #30	71
About the Author	73

family

Story Reflections

Story #1

"My shortcomings will help you evolve. You'll thank me later." No apologies, no acknowledgment that he had wronged me. I took offence to his arrogance and lack of sensibility.

"I need to travel for my studies, to improve my language skills." I had just given birth and he was back in school. Little did I know this was his exit plan.

"We are all one family, related by blood and kinship, forever united." I had agreed to marry him because I was certain he was the one.

"I can't wait for us to grow old together." Ten years of courtship, hesitation, trial, and error. That's how long it had taken for me to make a decision.

"I know the city well; may I help you find your way?"

How one fortuitous meeting can so profoundly derail your plans...

Story Reflections

Story #2

She has taken critical thinking to another level; nothing is as it seems. Such strength to question everything; it is eye-opening, refreshing. Perhaps because she loves to please, perhaps because she cares deeply. A reliable, trustworthy, dependable partner. No pressure. Remember, she does not have to be perfect, always searching for clues to improve the greater picture. A unique sense of humour, so personal to her. Absurdity and irony she will detect and expose. Obviously, not all will be amused. Her intuition is heightened, how accurately she detects the slightest divergence. Her comments are not always welcomed because of their laser precision. Her memory, linked to sounds and emotions; you can count on her if you tend to forget. Loving mother and faithful friend.

Story Reflections

Story #3

- Why does he always have to bring that wretched woman with him everywhere he goes?
- What else has she got to do with her life?
- —even when she knows she is not welcomed. I hate her for being so incapable of respecting herself. You, on the other hand, seem very good at being kind to her.
- Indeed, I don't have a problem. I didn't find her sitting on my bed as my husband stood by in his underwear.
- How kind of you to remind me of my misdirected resentment. I guess I should follow your example to keep my friends close and my enemies even closer.

Story Reflections

Story #4

She didn't fit in, and this shifted often, depending on the environment. Just for standing in the airport, one was automatically categorized as the diaspora. It wasn't her first visit, so she knew what impression she made. If she spoke, her accent revealed her status. If she remained silent, the locals would assume the same. Claiming to be offended was useless. She understood Creole—her knowledge and pronunciation, so rudimentary—she was, in fact, a foreigner. It would be easier for her to claim so, rather than search her genealogy. But only in the short term. You can't hide forever.

Story Reflections

Story #5

- Honey, it's supper time, please have a seat.
- I'm not hungry, I want to play.
- You can play afterwards, now we are going to eat.
- But I don't want to eat.
- You don't want to, or you can't? Do I need to feed you?
- My hands hurt; I can't use them.
- Should we go to the hospital to get them fixed?
- No!
- If you don't use your hands, you might lose them, and if you don't use your feet to get here, you might lose them too. If you lose your feet, then your bum bum might fall off, and if your bum bum falls off then you won't be able to sit.
- Then I don't have to eat!

Story Reflections

Story #6

The entire situation felt delusional. He never glanced in my direction and spoke of me in the third person as I sat directly in front of him at the dinner table. My mother then turned to me, repeated the question, and waited for an answer to transmit back to my father. Is he crazy? Am I? He had been a child once; did he not know that walls had ears and doors had mouths? Upstairs or in the basement, his low grumbling voice reverberated across the house. My brother says he does it on purpose so we can hear what he does not wish to say to our faces. Do I answer and validate the pathological triangle? Do I remain silent since I am not being spoken to? Do I stand up and curse to remind them of my presence? I only wish not to lose my mind.

Story Reflections

Story #7

Jack and Jill sat side by side in the waiting room while their children ran around noisily, adding to the irritation of the other patients. Only Jill seemed hot and flustered by their misbehaving, uselessly attempting to grab at one then the other to sit or quiet them down. To no avail. All eyes were on her, as though glancing at her repetitively would calm the children. The irresponsible parent, the bad mother. The more often she got up or gesticulated, the louder they got. Only seven and five, but already an unspoken dynamic and tension between them and their mother. The mother, who has no authority over them. Jack sits absentmindedly, unconcerned by the chaos, staring at the blank wall before him. Unconcerned, unaware; perhaps his mind is just as blank.

Story Reflections

Story #8

No one turns on the lights, even as the evening sets in. My mother, upright in the chair at the end of the room, eyes darting, lips pinched, ready to burst. My daughter sniffles on the couch next to her. I can hear my father ruffling papers in the other room. I feign ignorance. "What's the matter?" *The child is sick; it's all your fault. You are irresponsible... such a bad mother. You should know better and be at her side at all times. Where were you off to? What are your priorities? Don't you know how to raise a child?* The density of the silence is smothering. My mother, barely containing herself, aggressive, on edge. "NOTHING!" she yells.

Story Reflections

Story #9

We clumsily shoved everything in the car. The train was leaving in twenty minutes. I saw his grip tighten on the steering wheel; our short, ten-minute drive was too long at this very moment. We remained silent. I knew better than to chatter nervously this morning. This morning, which we had slept through because the baby kept us awake all night. This morning when the taxi did not show up on time. This morning, as I dashed out of the car, running through the parking lot, pressing the baby to my chest so as not to jolt him too much. This morning, my husband a few steps behind, struggling across the station, the luggage and infant car seat clunking against him as they shut the boarding doors in our faces.

Story Reflections

Story #10

"Were we talking to you?" I spat out the words and glared at my brother. I felt my jaw clench and my nostrils flare. I had inherited my dad's temper: when things don't go your way, express aggression in sudden spurts. Never be straightforward about what is bothering you. Always blame others. Remain defiant and inflexible. My brother had just completed a course in non-violent communication. Just the title irritated me. I took his attempt at learning healthier ways to communicate as a comment on my behaviour. Everything triggered me. The gurus and Zen communities I had been following did not seem to be improving my temper. I wondered if there was a way of meditating my attitude away. Maybe I could levitate myself into oblivion.

Story Reflections

Story #11

When I stood up at my cousin's wedding to tell the pastor his question to my twelve-year-old niece was inappropriate, I did not consider how my family might later shun me. When I condemned my adult sister for sneaking around with a teenage boy, I forgot this would further divide us. When I criticized my in-laws for taking up too much space and making decisions about raising my son, I later suffered from their lack of support. When I tried to run out of a restaurant without paying and got caught, I knew I would take this secret to my grave.

Story Reflections

Story #12

She sat at one end of the dinner table, closest to the door, beneath the burnt light bulb of the chandelier. They were all sharing a meal, but unlike the others, she was eating reheated leftovers because she had arrived late. On her left, her cousin and his partner were giggling quietly and snuggling together. In front of them, her aunt and grandmother were sustaining a conversation loud enough to include everyone and cover their discomfort. At the other end, another cousin was laughing when appropriate, lulled by the wine, affecting unease for drinking alone. She sat there, stoic, regretting accepting the invitation, wishing she could evaporate into the shadows.

Story Reflections

Story #13

I had explained this was a matter of life or death. He sat before me, avoiding my gaze, squirming in his seat. If he did not get his wife out of that country, he might never see her again. The immigration officer had not believed their story of how they met and later wed. He fumbled with his cell phone and mumbled inaudibly, then fell silent. I had given him a list of convincing evidence to gather before the appeal. He had just returned from visiting her in the refugee camp, and my expectations were as high as the stakes.

Twice he parted his lips, sighed, and retreated into himself, "I don't know if this is appropriate; if it counts as evidence." The silence dragged on. I understood he had not brought what I asked. It was starting to be embarrassing.

"I can prove she is my wife; I have a video." He slid his wedding band up and down his phalanx and opened an application on his phone. I watched his Adam's apple glide in and out as he turned the screen towards me.

Struggling to keep a straight face and hide my shock, I looked away. "No, I said, we can't use this."

work

Story Reflections

Story #14

I remember finishing my first year of university and feeling completely lost. I would wander, aimlessly, from one classroom to the next and wonder *how did I ever get here?* I would get good grades because that was expected of me.

In one of my last classes of the year, the professor invited public servants to present at a conference. I sat beside one of the presenters, and I mustered the courage to ask for a job. "Do you have a job for me?" Not, "Hello, how are you?" or "Hello, my name is ..." Simply, bluntly, "Do you have a job for me?" followed by the frozen smile of bad acting, the expectant glare of the naive. Was it my tactlessness, her powerlessness, my lack of decorum and ignorance of protocol, or her annoyance for being put on the spot that left her speechless? She sharply turned to me, like discovering a creature, alien to her and the surroundings, strange but nonthreatening, and just as quickly, she looked away.

Story Reflections

Story #15

She told me if I were not able to bill more clients, I would end up eating beans every day. This was before the plant-based fad. It could never occur to her that rice and beans were healthy staples for us. Her red meat diet showed off her wealth. She suggested I network and build a practice like hers. The outward signs of success.

How do you measure a successful life? Her advice was only as worthy as the desire to emulate her, of which I had none. So much power, so little understanding of the inner workings of the soul. Her unsolicited advice and material standards, a marked difference with my life choices. Perhaps meditation and spirituality were also fads. Looking inward is so much harder than attracting millions.

Story Reflections

Story #16

I remember younger, less experienced authors bemoaned the vicious competition of those they looked up to as mentors within the community. Who were we to turn to as we searched for guidance for our first scribbling attempts? Had it not been for my naïveté, I would have never started my career as a novelist. Ever since that first workshop on how to write a long story… Now, the description specifies the workshop is for seasoned writers, well advanced with their novel. The things we do when we are unaware… The workshop leader had sensed the participants' impatience and had even admitted in private, that kindness had slipped out the window. The other writers must have felt I was wasting their time, and yet, I persevered. I think a true leader would have intervened. But are writers leaders or even role models?

Story Reflections

Story #17

I often wonder how the status quo is advantageous to them. Do they genuinely believe the benefits of meritocracy can only befall a few? Samantha got hired on a part-time basis so she could keep her former job as a safeguard. As soon as she found something better, she claimed the initial terms of the contract were not good enough. Marie-Aure, the runner up, was more than willing to accept the terms and conditions, the novelty, the challenge. The ideas spurted from her mind, the excitement of the limitless opportunities to reach out to the community, offer much-awaited programs, shift structures and policies, question habits. Disrupt.

Story Reflections

Story #18

She was out for ten days straight with a congested sinus, a sore throat and a migraine. The cold smacked her full force across the head when the director announced that her friend, who she had recommended for the job, who had the strongest profile, the most lived experience, a résumé loaded with accomplishments and celebratory references, was not hired. Both friends were so convinced they would work together, they had already begun planning the yearly programming for members. When she finally got over her cold, she confronted him, citing poor judgment, questioning his intentions for the organization. He thought he was above reproach. After all, he had answered, his ex-wife was African.

Story Reflections

Story #19

There were three interviewers for this job, one of whom was joining virtually as if the situation was not already uncomfortable. It's always a bad idea to arrive unprepared. I was unprepared because I knew I did not want to be there. I answered candidly and politically incorrectly. I plastered a fake smile on my face and unsuccessfully attempted to lighten up the atmosphere with misplaced jokes. I squirmed on my chair and ignored the awkward silences. It was only during the written exam that suddenly, I got up and walked out, the cursor blinking on the screen.

Story Reflections

Story #20

I once left a job after six months to travel and volunteer in Central America. It was my first job after graduation and even though I was making more money than I knew what to do with, I preferred quitting. I think it looked good for the organization to have someone like me in that position. In total, we were only seven, but I had nothing to do. Sometimes my supervisor would sit in my office and talk to me for hours about utter nonsense. Not only would he bore me senseless, but I wondered if he had anything to do. Despite this, I felt like a fraud. Would he discover that I spent most of my working hours browsing online? Would he surprise me and find me snoozing in my chair? Would he question my unauthorized changes to my schedule? The place was driving me crazy. After a union meeting, a colleague confided in me that one employee was blacklisted for arriving late and leaving early. She was held by confidentiality, but her intense staring made me uncomfortable. I almost sheepishly asked if it was me but remained silent. I never found out who that person was.

life

Story Reflections

Story #21

- I thought all elite athletes practiced core strengthening.
- They do, and bodybuilding as well. It's practically a full-time job.
- Juggling many responsibilities at once... Most single moms manage that all the time.
- True. Even athletes in individual sports have a team supporting them.
- Same 24 hours, different income. I guess if parents believed in teamwork they would still be together.
- Forever is a long time when it isn't working.
- Well, you didn't build muscle in a day, did you?
- I am dependable, grounded and rock solid. As a child, my mother once sprained her wrist giving me a spanking.

Story Reflections

Story #22

That happened years ago. Years ago. And I somehow believe I could have said something to change the outcome. Today, I have the exact words I would have wielded, and I repeat them to myself constantly. Maybe, just maybe...

It reminds me of last month's incident, yet not all elements unfolded in the same order. Again, I did not speak up. How is it that I can remember with such precision every detail that determined the outcome of that relationship from so long ago, yet, in the present, I cannot remind myself to protect my space and save my energy? If it happened years ago, why is that insight so relevant to me today? Let me learn the lesson, but not be bogged down by the memory.

Story Reflections

Story #23

You hadn't stopped to reflect on why you refused to leave. You were simply scared to be uprooted, again. This time you would really be alone because in seven years the country had changed—lost friends, lost cultural references, lost resources. You pressed the fat of your hands into your eyes. What a disaster! What would you do? Your mind raced at full speed, your bottom lip twitched, the words echoing in your head. Being reactive and defiant did nothing to build a sympathetic case. Starting over as a single mom, you would only be more frightened, more exposed. No one could know this and express humanity for your case. No one to make an exception. No one, but the one who denounced you, could understand.

Story Reflections

Story #24

The line cracked and cackled. The automated recording said there were thirty-seven minutes available for the communication. Two hundred pesos should have given me an hour. It was as though the wireless had a brain whose cables were trying to untangle themselves from the dialed number. *Cannot compute, connection incomplete*, it seemed to tell me. I pushed the phone closer to my ear; it had been years since I tried to reach them. Does anyone even have landlines anymore? A tone. A second one. Would I beg for forgiveness, or jump for joy at the sound of their voices? I hadn't breathed. I gasped, surreptitiously, and held my breath again. Hello?

Story Reflections

Story #25

Speak your truth, they say. Listen with an open heart, don't hold back. Be transparent, honest and direct. Too bad if your explanation is unconvincing. Too bad if your comebacks are not on point. Too bad if they are a hit and miss. Don't expect to make a lot of friends though. The truth won't always make you popular. So, when is it ok to lie? When is lying an act of compassion and when is it a disservice? Are you concerned about people's unease or your own? Is it the desire to be right at all costs? Speak your truth they say, yet they are unwilling to hear it. Speak your truth, but beware of their unfurling rage.

Story Reflections

Story #26

How difficult is it to not gossip? How selective must one be? Whether to praise or condemn in the absence of the concerned one. Speaking of others, speaks mostly of us, for speaking of someone results from not speaking to that someone—that inalienable right to defend oneself. Rarely do we pause when praising or expressing love or holding back or rectifying. Only criticism and complaints are shunned as unsolicited and misdirected frustrations. Do your ears twitch, does your head buzz when you sense someone has been thinking of you?

Story Reflections

Story #27

"Well, I did my research," lips pressed, gaze averted, she nodded subtly to herself. That was her way of ending the conversation. Look no further. If the literature was worth perusing, she had exhausted every possible avenue on the topic. Never mind my beliefs, challenging her sources was not an option. If it's in a book, it must be the truth. The last time I disagreed with her, colour gradually tinted her face, a higher pitch in her voice. "Why not?" "How come?" Ready to pounce, regardless of my answers. So, I sat facing her and brought up the weather and how lovely her flowerbeds were blooming this year.

Story Reflections

Story #28

Even though I planned and organized the whole outing, he is going to tell me he is too busy. Then he will complain because the schedule I chose is not convenient. He will proceed to explain what I have already considered: leaving in the evening is too late, driving at night is dangerous, whitewater rafting is not a good idea. Is nothing else available? Where will we stop for food? Isn't there anything closer? I wasn't sure what was keeping me in this pattern. There was something about pleasing him. I thought he was so entitled to expect others to adjust to his preferences. Why was I doing this anyway?

Story Reflections

Story #29

Two words describe her: gluttony and greed. She eats twice as much as someone twice her size and has been known for fainting spells when hungry. She no longer 'cheaps' out on quality food and natural products, but still hesitates when it's time to split the bill— always wanting more, to fill a sense of void, a haunting feeling that there may never be enough. Do others comment on her table manners? Do they find them strange or distasteful? Does she eat too much or pay too little? What is fair? What seems right? Does it make a difference if she is alone, in the company of close friends, or with strangers? She often wonders if others spend as much as her on such trivialities. What is the social recipe for food and money?

Story Reflections

Story #30

As I handed her the fresh vegetables, I knew I would regret it. She grabbed them from me and set them on the counter, barely grunting. Though my guilt was misplaced, it motivated my gift. Her downcast eyelids and a discreet flinch of her lower lip told me that my gift would go unappreciated. It happened so rapidly. If I had taken the time to question her demand, my motivations and my need for love and acceptance, I would have loved myself first and not complied. I would have confronted her about her one-sided expectations. I would have held her accountable. I would like not to be so easily swayed.

About the Author

philippa c. jabouin has authored many articles and short stories under her name and as a ghostwriter. As a recovering ex-lawyer, she now spends her time writing as a freelance journalist, editor, and consultant. This is her first published collection of short stories. She lives in the Ottawa/Gatineau region of Canada.

CPSIA information can be obtained
at www.ICGtesting.com
Printed in the USA
BVHW030316090122
625753BV00001B/7

9 781777 972806